OMEGA ON THE RUN

MPREG Rejected Mate Romance

Michael Levi

CONTENTS

CHAPTER 1

Wadyn

"You can't keep running away from me," he taunted while I ran through the woods, trying to put as much distance between us as possible. My father turned my life into a living hell, and now I hated him as much as I hated the wolf coming after me.

He thought that we were fated mates, but that was just silly and there was nothing to do with reality.

Not to mention that I had just turned 19 and my entire pack wanted to match me to that wolf running through the woods after me, and I felt like no matter how much distance I put between us, he was going to find me one way or another.

Sweat covered my forehead, reminding me that I'd been running through these woods for what felt like an eternity. The Alpha should be right on my tail, considering that his smelling capabilities were unbelievably strong.

Stronger than mine, as they should be. After all, he was an Alpha, and Alphas like him, especially from the Darktail pack, were known for being excellent trackers.

Differently from most wolves, he was alone. He was chasing after me by himself because he wanted to claim me for himself, even though the mere notion of that happening was ridiculous, making me feel as though I was going to find myself in a ravine anytime now.

Considering that it was dark, the moon rising brighter and bigger in the sky, it was actually interesting that he hadn't transformed yet. I wonder if he was holding that back only because he didn't want to make this even easier than it was.

That was one of the reasons why my blood was boiling right now. I kept thinking that Yanric was toying with me, which wouldn't be too far-fetched, considering that he had to be much faster than me in any situation, including running through this forest.

The dark, tall trees surrounded me, making me feel smaller than I was. I was about a head shorter than Yanric and every time I was with him, I felt so exposed and submissive that it was maddening.

That was one of the other reasons why we could never end up together. Our relationship would never be fair, and he would always be the one on top, always being able to impose himself in any argument we had.

I just wasn't looking forward to that was what I was saying.

I ran past another big, tall tree when I tripped on something on the ground. I didn't even know what it was, just that my foot got stuck in it, and my body was in a moment spiraling out of control.

The first thought that crossed my mind was that I was going to hit my head against one of the trunks before losing consciousness, but I actually managed to avoid that by pushing myself back from the tree looming in front of me.

But it didn't help me much, considering that my body was still falling over, and upon glancing down, I noticed that there was a huge hole in the ground, which was actually a ravine.

Just like I thought it was going to happen, Yanric was going to find me and capture me, and then he would have me exactly where he wanted me. I could already hear his voice in my head, and I was certain that he was going to have a lot to say to me.

After all, I was making such a fool of myself.

I could already picture Yanric saying that stuff about knotting me or whatever it was. It was gross. He wanted to be inside of me.

Just thinking about that, I felt such a repulsion in me it was difficult to control it, and while I still fell deeper into the ravine, the ground and debris hurting me, I knew that from this moment onward I would never be able to walk anywhere again, and that was putting it mildly.

"Oh, shit," Yanric said the moment he arrived at the top of the ravine, looking down at me and seeming more desperate about this than I thought he could show.

I never thought that he cared so much about me that his eyes were going to be filled with worry upon seeing me falling into the ravine. But it wasn't like I had much time to see what else his face was displaying, considering that my body was still spinning into the ravine, and I would be lucky if I got out of this alive, to say the least.

Still thinking that, I groaned and puffed out all the air in my lungs when my back hit something big and hard at the bottom of the ravine, making me lose, at least temporarily, the capability to feel anything that touched my body, and that was putting it mildly.

I looked up, finding it difficult to turn my neck while my nose sniffed the Alpha standing on top of the ravine, glaring down at me as though he was planning on finishing the job.

And by that, I meant killing me.

I wasn't going to deny that he looked a little imperious and hot, his body shining under the moonlight. He was fit, no denying it. Before I learned the kind of person that he truly was, I thought that we would have sex and, er, he would even knot me.

It was a good thing that those things weren't going to happen anymore.

After all, I was dying. No denying it. I could feel my life slipping away, and there was nothing I could do about it. Trying to move my arms and legs to stand up and run away from here and I found out how pointless that was.

I couldn't say this for real, but it felt like I'd broken my spine. Perhaps it could be even worse, but I couldn't tell that from just trying to feel my back, which I couldn't do right now at all.

Either way, Yanric decided to do something stupid, or maybe

it was actually pretty smart. He jumped down into the ravine, sliding down the slope.

"Hang on, I'm coming for you," he announced, making me feel shivers running down my spine.

He might be using this moment to try to show me he wasn't as bad as I thought, but I knew better. I knew that he was going to use it to knot me – even without my consent.

That was how bad it was, I thought.

"Stay away from me," I barked, but he shook his head the moment he landed at the bottom of the ravine.

"When are you finally going to learn that you need me even when you think you don't?" He asked, putting his arms under me and lifting me, supporting me with his body.

I could tell that from the way he was looking at me, supporting me like this wasn't difficult for him at all, and that was putting it mildly.

This wolf was so much bigger than me and he probably weighed twice as much as I did.

I could feel his hard, sculpted muscles with my arm and the side of my body, which was at least something positive about this. Even though I had promised myself I would never touch him again, it was good to know that my body still felt things. It was still capable of doing that, which meant that I wasn't in a completely desperate situation.

"I hate you so fucking much, Yanric," I growled, wishing that I was a wolf as well so that I could transform and overpower Yanric with everything I had.

And yet, my body responded differently. It was like the whole fated mates thing was truly real even though I thought it was bullshit.

I actually wanted to be in the city and not in the woods, where we had to be hiding away from everybody while pretending that we could keep living like nomads without it feeling weird.

That was how I looked at it, at least.

"And yet, you now need my help more than ever before in your life, and I know that means you are going to spend a lot of time with me, more so than you ever thought you would," he explained, smirking.

Of course that Yanric was going to be smirking, knowing that I couldn't run away now.

Still, there was a sense of safety, being with him like this right now. I didn't want to accept it, so I just shunned it, and nothing was going to change my mind about that.

No matter how much my cock swelled while I felt his strong scent coming from his body...

"Up we go," he said before shooting up with me to the top of the ravine. He moved so fast that we were like a thunderbolt, and I never thought that he could be so nimble, too.

He moved as though he was trying to tell me that, when he was chasing me, he was actually only toying with me.

That was another reason why my blood boiled in rage right now.

CHAPTER 2

Yanric

Oh boy. Wadyn was going to keep making this hard for me, even though he had such a huge turn-on for me that, quite frankly, he couldn't control it anymore.

He was almost passing out, though.

I told him that there was no point in running away from me, but he was still so stupid and stubborn. To be honest, I was feeling a little bad, considering that I should have been able to stop him before he fell into the ravine.

His spine ended up hitting a trunk at the bottom, almost breaking it. It didn't happen, though, considering that he was still able to mostly keep himself straight, even though right now he had to be supporting himself on my body.

That was something he hated, though. No denying it. If it were up to him, this wouldn't be happening at all.

I felt the warmth coming from his body, but it was his scent that confirmed my suspicions. He was my fated mate, and there was no denying it.

As much as he thought that it wasn't the case, my dick swelled thinking about him and I being together, and I just wanted to make us happen so much.

"Where the fuck are you taking me?" He asked, his eyes glaring at me.

"The place where you should be. I told you that running away from me was pointless, and now you can see that I was completely right about it."

"Whether you were right about it or not, I don't care. All I care about is that I don't want to be with you, no matter how much you are trying to show me that things can be different. And no matter how nice you try to seem to me, you will never knot me."

I smirked. "We'll see about that," I taunted, making him feel even more rage toward me. I felt that no matter how much I tried to make myself look better for him, he always thought that I was the worst wolf in the pack.

I was a watchman and we didn't have much in common. We talked a little before all this, but that was really all the interaction we had together before his father also came to the same conclusion.

He told me that I was to marry Wadyn.

When he told me that, I felt that my suspicions about Wadyn being my fated mate were all true. After all, it was one thing for an Alpha to suspect that of an Omega that, and another to hear the confirmation straight from the person that knew Wadyn so well.

I wasn't lying about it. That was exactly what happened.

"Take me back home," he pleaded, making me roll my eyes.

"You want to be taken back home? Didn't you say that you hated your father so much that you don't even want to see him again?"

"You don't know anything about me. I just don't want to be in your village with your pack, no matter how much you are trying to be nice right now."

"Oh boy, you really don't know anything about me. The problem is that you need a healer right now and, in your village, you don't have one. That's why I'm taking you to my place. My father is a healer and he will look after you."

"I don't want to be looked after. I just want to be left alone."

"Wadyn, if I leave you alone right now, you will die. Is that what you really want?" I asked, watching his reaction while still dragging ourselves through the forest and in the direction of my village.

If he thought that I was going to take him to his father's village, then he was going to be disappointed. No matter what else he said to me, he just couldn't change my mind about it.

"No, I suppose not," he responded a couple of minutes later after thinking about his answer for what felt like an eternity.

He weighed like nothing right now, and my dick just couldn't stop swelling. I knew that Wadyn was cute and all, but thinking about him sexually right now was just wrong.

"See?" I said, still making our way back to my village. "I knew that you were going to see reason."

He scoffed. "See reason?" He asked, sounding dumbfounded by it. "You don't really have any idea about what's going on here and what I'm really thinking."

"Oh, really?" I asked, deciding to be a little bold right now. "And what is it about you that I'm not quite getting right now?"

He pouted, turning his head the other way.

"I'm not going to say anything else."

A moment of silence between us. I couldn't help but wonder if I should make the question that nagged my mind about it right now.

Licking my bottom lip, I said, "have you ever dated before?"

He snapped his eyes to me, looking awestruck by my question.

"What sort of question is that?" He asked, sounding more surprised by it than he should be. "I'm not going to answer."

"You're not going to answer me because you feel ashamed of it, right?"

"That's just stupid," he grumbled, stepping with me over a small trunk fallen on the ground. We could hear the crickets chirping and the owls hooting, reminding us that we were still in the woods. It was going to take some time until we got out of here, to say the least. "See? It's because of what you are doing right now and so many other moments that I hate you so much."

I shook my head, deciding that it just wasn't worth it.

"You do realize that I could go for pretty much anyone else, right?" I asked, making it pretty clear what was going on here. I was only going after this Omega because I really thought that he was the one I needed.

"Then, why? Why aren't you nagging somebody else?"

I chuckled. "Wadyn, you keep making this so difficult even though it's so pointless."

Either way, there was no point in continuing this conversation with him right now. Not the topic we were discussing, anyway.

"Since you are going to be living with me for a while now until you make up your mind about the truth regarding us, then I think we should do everything possible to accommodate you in my hut."

"Accommodate me?" Wadyn asked, making me roll my eyes.

"Obviously. Like I told you, I'm actually kinder than you thought, so I want to make sure that you are going to feel at home when we arrive."

"I still didn't say that I actually want to be taken to your village."

I stopped moving with him, the wind swirling around us.

"If that's not what you want, then what? Where do you want to be taken? Spit it out now before I lose my patience with you," I growled, my body growing warmer and my fur showing.

Shit. By doing that, I was showing that Wadyn wasn't wrong about me. After all, he thought that I was violent and prone to rage outbursts.

So, I took a deep breath and calmed myself down.

Nothing was going to ruin this moment we were sharing.

"You were angry at me again," he pointed out as though it was something that needed to be explained. I mean, of course it was obvious. I ran through the woods, chasing him even though I could have just ignored him and thought that we could never be lovers.

But I just really wanted to give ourselves a chance.

"Of course I was. Despite helping and saving you, you are still saying the same shit to me, and honestly, sometimes it can get infuriating."

He looked down, seeming sorry about the way he acted.

"I'm sorry if I sounded ungrateful about you helping me right now. I still hate you with passion, but at least you are doing something good, taking me to your village and your father. I'm sure he's a great healer."

I blinked twice, for a moment not understanding that he was capable of showing me he was wrong about something.

I had always thought that Wadyn was too self-centered and proud of himself for his own good. I never thought he was going to say that.

Chuckling, I said, "I suppose it's okay. Don't worry about it. Just tell me everything you need to feel better when we arrive, and then we will send a letter to your dad and tell him what happened. I'm sure he will be ecstatic to know that you are okay. Even though you hate him, he still cares about you."

And I was right. His dad cared about him, and probably as much as I did.

CHAPTER 3

Wadyn

I just never thought it was going to happen, me lying in this bed and looking up at the ceiling of the hut. My body hurt like hell, but at least it was a good thing that it felt that. Otherwise, if I wasn't feeling anything, it would be really so bad for me.

It would be much worse than pretty much anything that could be healed.

"I'm going to get my father," Yanric announced, staying at the entrance of the hut and looking at me as he waited to see my reaction. I nodded and he bolted out, already shouting so that everyone could hear him. Even if his father was in a completely different place, he would have already heard his shouts.

I didn't like his father. There was bad blood between us, and there was nothing I could do about that.

I sighed, wishing that I could at least roll over on my back and bury my head in the pillows. They weren't great. They came from the continent, where people lived in the big cities and drove fast, fancy cars.

I wanted that life instead of living for the rest of my life on this island, wondering what was going to happen when I didn't have enough strength to do the things I needed to do.

But it was all something for another time.

Time must have passed a lot faster than I thought. When I

thought I was falling asleep, I heard his voice booming from the entrance of the hut.

I'd seen people living in the big cities, in the rare opportunities I watched TV, and I wanted that. I didn't want this boring, mundane life here on this island infested with bugs and all sorts of other creatures.

Not to mention getting pregnant and having to start a family just because my father wanted me to.

Anyway, I needed to be focusing on what was happening here, and that was the older man standing in the doorway, who was holding something in his hand. It was a small first-aid kit, which was funny. I thought that he was going to bring something a lot bigger than that red box, considering he was supposed to be the 'healer' in here.

'Healer.'

Thinking about that, I couldn't help but chuckle. A healer. On the continent, he would be called a scammer, but here, people looked up to him.

I guess that that was mostly because of his calm and controlled demeanor, that aura that surrounded him.

"Did you really have to do that?" He asked, pulling a chair and sitting on it. Really? Was he really going to act as though he was my father? And what about Yanric? What the hell did he think he was doing that he couldn't come here now?

I kind of yearned for his presence.

"I don't know what you are talking about," I replied after much consideration. If you thought that I was going to admit he was right, then he was going to disappoint himself.

He was an Omega just like I was and was the one that gave birth to Yanric. He was a strong advocate for this 'culture' on the island, and it churned my stomach.

"I think you know exactly what I'm talking about," he said, his eyes scanning me. "And I can see that you are in pretty bad shape. Whatever you thought you were doing running away, it didn't work. You only managed to get yourself hurt, and now here you are needing my help again."

"You don't know anything about me," I growled, once more wishing that I could transform just so that I could slap his face and make him admit that everything he thought about me was wrong.

"Actually, I know a lot about you. As you know, I'm an Omega like you are, and I know that you're thinking you have a lot of dreams going out there into the continent, but let me tell you this: the moment you set foot in there, those people will destroy you. They don't think you are like them and they think it's 'weird' that a man like you can get pregnant. Your cubs will be hated and shunned."

My cubs? What the hell did he think he was talking about? I didn't imagine myself getting pregnant, and I didn't want any sexual relationship with anyone. Everything that I wanted right now was just to have my own place, a nice backyard for weekend barbecues, and peace. Nothing more than that.

It was obvious that this Omega, who lived here his whole life and was brainwashed by his own father, couldn't understand me.

Either way, he came here to heal me - the thing that he was supposed to do as a healer - and that was exactly what he was going to do, and I hoped that he was going to be quick about it.

I didn't want to interact much more with him.

"I'm not thinking about that," I affirmed, taking a deep breath. "Actually, the only thing I want right now is for you to heal me, and I hope that's exactly what you're going to do."

He took a deep breath, obviously trying to calm himself down. "Fine. I'm not doing this for you, but for Yanric. He loves you. You might think that's not the case, but he loves you even more than me, and I hate that," he said, his eyes locked with me.

Gosh. I found myself stuck in this situation and there was nothing I could do about it. My rage was impotent and I hated him as much as I hated myself.

Minutes later, he finally finished doing everything he could. Obviously, without the proper equipment and only being a healer, most of his healing came in the form of 'potions.' He made me drink so much stuff it made me feel like I was drunk or high, or maybe both things at the same time.

Either way, it was just weird, and I passed out before long. At least I didn't have to hear his voice anymore, which was pretty great, now that I was thinking about it.

And... There was one more thing that I wanted to do, which was to not have nightmares about marriages and carrying a kid in my belly. Every time that I thought about that, my stomach churned.

***

Waking up, I was surprised to find Yanric on the other side of the hut, preparing something on a table. What that was, I couldn't even begin to guess. I did find myself eyeing him, something that I should be feeling ashamed of, considering my history of antagonizing him.

Time passed and nothing happened. I couldn't help but wonder what he was doing, though I could hear the soft rustling of something. Perhaps he was handling some pieces of clothing? I didn't know, but it was intriguing.

Plus, he was handsome, his back wide and stretchy, his shirt clinging to it like it didn't want to leave and was glued. Sometimes, I wished I was doing the same just because he would make me feel safe, not to mention me resting my head on his chest, feeling the warmth coming from his body.

Something like that would never happen, and I should keep that in mind, no matter how much he made my cock swell.

It was so hard right now I was happy that I had a blanket and it covered my body, hiding my boner. Still, there was no denying that my scent was changing, and someone like Yanric had to be noticing that right at this moment.

Just thinking that, I felt uncomfortable and embarrassed.

"I know you are awake," he said, turning around as he held something in his hand. It was a shirt. It was plain yellow and looked pretty new, which was unusual for anything on this island. Most of the time, everything around here came from the continent and they were used and discarded stuff.

"So? I suppose you should be happy that I didn't kill myself. Sometimes, I think that might be the only and best thing I can do."

His eyes narrowed slightly, showing me that he didn't like my words.

"You know that joking about that isn't funny."

I sighed, realizing how ridiculous it was to get a sermon from Yanric. I mean, really? He'd been the bully back in school, nagging and tormenting pretty much everyone, and now he was trying to lecture me about suicide?

Give me a break.

"Whatever," I grumbled, holding my arms over my chest. The only positive thing going on right now was that I wasn't feeling as much pain as before. Did the 'healer' really manage to do it with all of his potions and everything else? If that was the case, then he should go to the continent and tell them how revolutionary his medicine was.

CHAPTER 4

Look, I came here with just one purpose in mind, which was to give him a change of clothes. So, I was hoping that he could at least stand up on his own and move his body without problems. Or else I would have to dress him up myself, and even though part of me was looking forward to that, I still didn't want to do it.

It was more than obvious that Wadyn didn't like me, and I had no idea what to do to change that.

No idea, really? I thought, smiling without showing my teeth. Actually, I did have some plans and I was going to put them into practice.

Me changing him just might be the opportunity I was looking for, even though part of me loathed it.

We just didn't have much in common other than the fact that I had this strong, incessant feeling in me that he was my fated mate. Everything just got so much more intense when his father confirmed my suspicions.

"Saying 'whatever' isn't going to change anything," I said, holding the plain yellow shirt in my hand. It was new, or almost as new as anything on this island could be. After all, everything we got here came from the continent.

He didn't say anything, just pouting and looking away. Really, when I first met Wadyn, I thought that he was much more cowardly, but now I could see how wrong about that I was. When there was something he didn't approve of, he always did everything in his power to show his displeasure.

I took a deep breath, chuckling – or at least holding back my chuckle. Again, it was imperative that I didn't do anything that pissed him off any more than he already was.

He turned his head to look at me again, saying, "so, what are you going to do now? Are you going to force me to like you?" He was taunting me and I wasn't going to fall into his trap. Doing that would be just stupid.

"I'm not going to do that. What I'm going to do is give you this shirt, my older shorts, and underwear. You are going to love putting them on. I know this is kind of weird, but you don't need to feel so much repulsion about it."

"I don't feel repulsion for anything. I just hate you. That's all that's really going on here," he affirmed.

"Look, I know we don't have much in common, but I'm glad we are talking. It allows us to get to know each other better and I know that's exactly what you think, too," I said, going straight to the point.

After a while, I noticed that Wadyn wasn't willing to say anything.

That was fine.

"So, do you want to try my shirt? I know that you are going to love it," I said, finding it impossible to erase my smile.

"I'm not going to put that on," he shouted, showing his anger.

I cocked my head, shrugging. "If you don't want it, then I suppose there really is nothing we can do and you are going to keep smelling bad until your dad comes."

For an Omega, that was terrible. His nose was just too sensitive.

"I don't have to wear your stuff. I don't care about this. I just want to… Look, I don't really know what I want anymore. Maybe I just want to be left alone, like I said I wanted even before all of this happened."

"Well, you can't be left alone." I took a deep breath in, still holding the shirt. Alright, this was more like a matter of honor to me at this point, and my goal right now was to make him put on the shirt. I was certain that he would look good in it even if it was a size too big. "Can you even move without feeling too much pain?"

He tried to move his arm up, but then grimaced, showing me just how much pain he was feeling.

"See?" I asked, taunting him. "You can't go anywhere and even after your father comes here, he will agree that you need to stay here for the time being. Remember that he also thinks you are my fated mate."

"I'm not your mate and much less fated to be your husband. I don't know what you are thinking is going to happen, but the moment I feel better, I will leave and you will never see me again."

Chuckling, I said, "we'll see about that."

There was a moment of silence, with neither of us daring to say anything. There were plenty of things I wanted to say, but I was going to keep my lips sealed for now about them, deciding to do that when the time was right. "So, your current clothes are dirty and you need at least a new shirt. You can't even move your body without grimacing. Don't you want me to put my shirt on you?"

Wadyn widened his eyes, showing me how much he didn't want to let that happen.

"I'm not going to let you do that. It's just ridiculous. Now you are treating me like I'm a baby."

"Well, you are not a baby, but you certainly need someone to look after you," I said, going over to him and sitting on the bed. The mattress sagged with my weight.

"I'm still not changing my mind about it."

"Are you really not?" I insisted, pinching my own nose. There was a stench in the air coming from his dirty clothes, and it was another reason why he needed to put the shirt on at least. If not that, then I would leave him and walk out of the hut. I would still come back later for more, though. After all, I wasn't someone to give up so easily.

Another moment of silence hung in the air like something

mean and unforgiving. After a while, he turned his head, looking at me and then at the plain yellow shirt I was still holding.

"Fine, but I'm going to put it on myself."

"It's good progress that you have changed your mind about putting on the shirt, but it's not enough. Like you showed me, you can't even move your arms. My father did enough to make you feel better, but it will still take you some more time to heal."

"Your father is a scammer. He calls himself a healer, but he is nothing more than someone that makes other people think that he can actually heal them. On the continent, he would be no one."

I could let that get under my skin, but I wasn't going to do that. I knew that Wadyn was only trying to rattle me, and it wasn't going to work.

"You can say whatever you want about my dad, but it doesn't change anything. He managed to heal you, isn't that right?" I asked, studying his facial expression.

He bit his bottom lip, looking down at his hands.

"I know that expression. You are telling me, even though you are still trying to pretend that's not the case, that it's not like that. My father came here with good intentions, just like me."

"God, you are insufferable," Wadyn grumbled, throwing his arms up and grimacing, a brief scream of pain following.

"As I told you, you really need someone to put the shirt on you," I insisted, holding it out in front of me. After that, Wadyn took a deep breath, and it appeared that he was going to change his mind about what I wanted as well.

"Do you promise not to tell anyone about this?" He asked, his eyes trembling and watering. Wait, why was he crying right now? I asked myself, finding this weird and curious at the same time. I never thought that Wadyn would be crying, considering that he was always angry at me for every possible reason he could scrounge up. It was always anger and not… sadness.

"I promise not to tell anyone about this," I said and it was true. I wasn't going to tell anyone about it, even though it was kind of funny. I never thought that he cared so much about what other people would think about this.

"Fine, then you can put the shirt on me," he said and I lowered his blanket, revealing his body.

A sudden, obtrusive thought that crossed my mind right now was if he'd ever even kissed. Considering how his father was, he might have never done it. He wanted to keep Wadyn pure for the right Alpha.

But that was something for another time. For the time being, I was focusing on not fucking this up.

"You look so handsome, Wadyn," I said and it was true. He rolled his eyes, though, seeming annoyed even though his scent told me a different story. It told me that he actually wanted this even though he was annoyed at himself, too, and probably a lot more than he was at me.

"You shouldn't be saying those things. It's not appropriate."

CHAPTER 5

Wadyn

And it really wasn't. I didn't know what was going on in Yanric's mind, but his comment on my looks was just inappropriate even though it stirred something different in me, something that I shouldn't be feeling, especially not for him.

I mean, what the hell was I even thinking I would do with my life when I was on the continent? Would I date someone else? Would I date a normal... human?

I didn't know, but he would certainly give me something better than this; a life that couldn't progress and would never go anywhere. It was imperative that I left my family and this life as fast as I could, not wanting to fall into the trap that awaited me.

"I know you liked it."

"I don't know what you're talking about," I grumbled, keeping my arms folded over my chest – and at least this was something I could do without it hurting too much. The more I thought about it, the more I hated this moment. I couldn't even put my shirt on and it made me feel pathetic.

It was all true. I hated Yanric so much right now that I wouldn't hesitate before opening a huge hole in his neck... If only I could do that.

"I think you know exactly what I'm talking about," he pointed out, accentuating the words. He knew how to get on my nerves, and it was working. And the worst thing was that it was showing in my scent.

"Anyway, time to take off your shirt," he said, sliding his fingers under it, and I felt them gliding on my belly. It made me feel something alien, something that swelled my dick, and I didn't know how to react to that.

Actually, scratch that. I knew how to react. I had to react by not doing anything and trying to change my scent as much as I could, even though doing so felt impossible.

His eyes locked with mine. It was as if he was asking for permission, which was just dumb. He had it. I'd already said he could take off my shirt.

Still, he was going to see my exposed torso, and I hoped that he wasn't going to laugh at it. After all, his torso was so completely different from mine. It was like it had been sculpted by the gods, and that was putting it mildly.

The gods... Thinking about them, I couldn't help but feel disdain. I didn't know why people still revered them, and why they still thought they existed.

Anyway, I shouldn't be going off on a tangent, thinking that this was all going to change. It wasn't going to.

Eventually, he slid the shirt up a little bit, but there was something different about it, something that I didn't want to think was there, but which still was. He took his time doing that, and he made sure that he touched the skin of my belly as much as possible without making it weird.

Without making it weird? Scratch that. It was already so, and I couldn't do anything about it.

Then, he grabbed my arms, lifting them up. I noticed the way he was touching them, and I couldn't quite put my finger-

Oh, come on. I knew exactly what was going on in his mind. He was touching my arms and holding them with absolute care and love while, at the same time, being controlling and determined.

He truly looked at me as his soul mate.

Eventually, he finished sliding the shirt up and pulled it off me, his eyes scanning my torso. I could fold my arms over my chest again, but what would be the point? It wasn't like it would change much, considering that he was already seeing everything.

And what was that in the air? I asked myself, noticing the difference in his scent. Was it really telling me that he felt the same way I felt? Was he really turned on by looking at me?

My exposed chest?

That was dumb. There was nothing special with my chest and I was being kind to myself about it.

"What?" I asked, hoping that it was going to bring him back to reality. For a moment, he was just really studying my chest, his fingers doing something I couldn't quite describe. It was like he was doing everything in his power not to touch me, even though he wanted to do that so much.

Yanric cleared his throat, trying to save face.

"Sorry. I was just caught up by your striking looks."

"Shut up. Just put the shirt on me already. I'm feeling cold," I said, being slightly truthful about that. I was indeed feeling a little cold, even though I actually didn't want to say anything about it. I was worried that he was going to be concerned about that and consider snuggling up to me. Maybe he would even spoon me just to keep me warm, even though it would be ridiculous, even more so than everything that happened before now.

Smiling devilishly, he replied, "yeah, don't worry. I'm going to do that right away, *boss*."

"I'm not your boss-" I was saying the moment he grabbed my arms again, holding them up gently to not hurt me. Again, there was that softness in his touch, and I really felt that he was doing everything in his power to not hurt me. Maybe he felt bad for chasing me in the woods, but I couldn't know that for sure.

Just like last time, he made sure to touch me as much as he could and make it last as much as possible. His scent was changing, too, which could only mean one thing.

Yanric really was in love with me, or at least he thought he was.

Did that matter, though?

"There. You already look a lot better with my shirt," he said, rubbing that in my face. He was boasting about his victory, and it infuriated me so much. Why did he have to be doing this?

I glanced down, not wanting to admit that the shirt kind of looked good on me, even if only slightly better than my other one. Even though it wasn't my favorite one, it was one of the shirts I liked, and that was putting it mildly.

"Shut up."

"Well, you will still have to put on the pants and the underwear I got for you."

"You know, since we are savages living on this island, I wonder why we have to wear anything at all."

He blinked twice in a row, for a moment not understanding what I meant.

"You mean you want to walk around naked?" He asked, standing up.

I looked to the side, my cheeks flushing beet-red. "Something like that. Sometimes I wonder what it would be like to enjoy the beauties of this island without all the negative things getting in the way."

"You're crazy," he said, chuckling. He padded over to the other side of the hut, grabbing the pants. It was a pair of jeans. I knew that from the movies I'd watched, I remembered.

Shaking my head, I said, "I don't want to wear that right now, and it doesn't matter how much you try to change my mind about it – it won't work."

He put it back down on the small table.

"Fine. If you don't want to wear it, there's nothing I can do about it. Still, I think you're still going to be pretty smelly even with my shirt on."

I bit my bottom lip. I just didn't want what would happen if he were to put the shirt on me. He would see me naked.

"Why don't we wait a little while longer until I can move my body more freely?" I asked, pointing out the obvious.

"Do you really want to wait?" Yanric asked, for a moment sounding disappointed.

I nodded. There was just really nothing else to do. No chance that Yanric was going to see me naked. At least, not this morning.

"I just don't want… You know," I said under my breath, trying to hide it as much as possible. I mean, what else was I going to say? Should I say that I didn't want him to see me naked?

Sometimes, Yanric could be so dense, but not this time.

His eyes cleared up. "Of course. No problem with that, at least not to me."

After saying that, he padded over to the entrance of the hut, pushing the flannels up.

Then, he winked.

He fucking winked!

I couldn't believe it.

CHAPTER 6

Yanric

Coming back to the hut, I thought that I was going to find him sleeping. And, he kind of was. But he was only trying to fool me, which was silly. Wadyn wasn't sleeping, but pretending. I mean, I'd seen the way that he threw his body the other way, rolling over on the bed.

The bed and the mattress all came from the continent. The more I thought about it, the more I realized that Wadyn was kind of right about it.

We needed them, and it would be kind of interesting to travel over there. Still, we didn't think that it would ever happen, considering that people there would mistreat us a lot more than sometimes it already happened here.

"Wakey, wakey," I joked, trying to be casual about this.

What he thought wasn't going to change who I was, and I was going to do everything in my power to soften his heart for me. Before he knew it, he was going to be begging to be in my arms.

"I know you aren't sleeping," I insisted, but he remained doing exactly the same thing he was doing. Still with his back turned to me, the blanket covering his body, not moving at all.

How interesting.

He was really going to make this difficult for me, wasn't he? I asked myself, padding over to him. Stopping behind him, I moved my hand, looking for his armpit. If there was something that I knew about Wadyn, it was that he was very ticklish.

And I could take advantage of that.

But just before I could touch his armpit, he spun around under the blanket, his eyes meeting me. I knew he was going to do that, so I wasn't surprised by it. I was slightly taken aback by it, but that was unimportant right now.

Putting my hands on my waist, I said, "I knew you were going to do it."

"Yeah, whatever," he said, sitting up on the bed and I realized he was able to do that without grimacing. I wondered if that meant he was mostly healed now. If that was the case, then I had to hurry up.

The moment he didn't need me anymore, he would certainly leave and all the progress we were developing so far would amount to nothing.

Sniffing the air in front of me, I said, "you still stink. Are you really sure that you don't want to change your pants... and underwear as well?"

His eyes widened; his surprise palpable. "I'm not going to do that! I don't even know what you think you're doing here. I already told you I don't need your help anymore, plus I'm starting to feel better already."

"Still, not good enough to take a shower and change your clothes by yourself, right?" I asked even though it was obvious.

Pouting and averting my gaze, he said, "you are wrong about that."

"No, I'm not," I insisted, letting time pass and, this time, Wadyn didn't say anything. He was really doing everything in his power to seem tougher than he really was, wasn't he?

It wasn't that I was downplaying that or anything of the sort. After all, Wadyn was tough as nails, but I still thought that the path he was following was only hurting him.

"There's something about you I want to ask," I said, feeling that we were getting more intimate, even though I could be wrong about it. Still worth a shot, anyway.

"What about?" He asked, his eyes looking at me and the different thing about this moment was that he didn't even try to avert his gaze. It was as though he wanted to confront me about whatever I wanted to ask him about.

"Have you ever kissed before? Are you still… pure?" I asked.

It was important to me. If he had already been taken by another Alpha, I would still do everything in my power to marry him and convince him that he was my fated mate, but it would be different, too.

"What sort of question is that?" He asked, folding his arms over his chest, and this time he didn't grimace. Good. He was really healing. My father was no scammer and he should admit that.

"The sort of question you should answer," I insisted, his eyes locked with mine.

I wasn't going to lie. This was a tense moment between us and I wondered how he was going to take it, all things considered.

"No, I'm not going to answer that question. It's just stupid," he barked, turning his eyes away from mine. Still, I could tell that there was something with my question that hit him differently. He didn't want to talk about it and that was fine, but I still wanted to hear his answer, no matter what it was.

"Are you not?" I asked, prodding the topic a little more. After all, I wasn't one to give up.

"If I say I kissed another Alpha, how would you feel about it?" He asked, his eyes still looking in the other direction. I felt that no matter how much I insisted on the subject, he was going to remain stubborn about not telling me anything about it, which I hated.

Still, Wadyn was going to come around, eventually.

"If you did that, it would be okay. Really, there would be nothing I could say about it. After all, you already hate my gut."

He chuckled. "You're right about that. You can't believe how much I hate you."

"You hate me so much, but every time I step into this hut, I notice the change in your scent, and it's pretty telling."

"Again, I don't know what you're talking about-" he insisted, but I raised my hand, cutting him off.

Every time we talked about a difficult topic, he always said he didn't understand what I was talking about. Come on, Wadyn wasn't stupid.

"Just stop saying that. It's not helping you and it only makes you look worse. To my eyes, at least."

He took a deep breath, eventually saying, "do you... promise me you won't tell anyone about it?"

I placed my hand on my chest. "Don't worry about it. My lips are sealed. It can be another secret between us."

"Alright," he said, taking a deep breath. He thought it was going to be a bombastic revelation, but I was already suspecting that my thoughts about it were right. "I've never actually kissed anyone."

A moment of silence between us. Wadyn wasn't even looking at me. His scent changed again, and I knew he was uncomfortable. So much so that he couldn't help but slide down the blanket, though without showing his boner.

I couldn't see it, but I knew that it was there and that he wished he didn't have to be hiding it anymore. What's more, he probably wished he could jack off.

To be honest, I wished I was doing that for him. Such a pity I couldn't...

"See?" He asked, still not looking at me. "I knew you were going to find it shameful."

"I don't know what you're talking about. I don't find it shameful. I actually find it cute," I said, being careful with my words.

"You find it cute?" Wadyn asked, finally snapping his head at me. "You've got to be fucking with me."

"Trust me. I'm not fucking with you," I affirmed, leaning in and feeling his smell, which was stronger and more acidic this time. It made me want to take the virginity of his mouth. If only I could do that, hmm...

A moment of silence between us, and I studied his eyes, asking myself what they were telling me right now. There were plenty of things he wanted to say, but he could only clear his throat.

Plus, his scent kept on changing, showing me that he was thinking the same thing.

"Err, what do you think you're doing?" He asked, still blushing.

"Do you want me to do something about that?" I asked, keeping my voice sexy and low.

"About what?" He asked. The more his scent changed, the more I thought I was certain about this.

God. My fated mate wanted me to kiss him, and I was going to do so much more than that, too.

"About your mouth problem," I said and he swallowed hard, not telling it to me with words, but still making it pretty obvious.

He wanted me to make out with him.

And it just might happen.

The problem was, I was only going to do it if he gave me another sign that he wanted to make it happen.

A deep breath and I knew it was going to happen.

CHAPTER 7

Uhhh, what the fuck did I think I was doing? I asked myself, noticing that his lips were getting closer. If I didn't stop this before it was too late, we would kiss for sure and… That would be the end of me.

I mean, how else would I be able to continue saying that I didn't like Yanric even though he was incredibly hot and persuasive. How else would he have been able to convince me he could put the shirt on me?

His eyes blinked one last time, assessing what I was thinking, and then… I just couldn't stop it anymore. His lips connected to mine, and I couldn't do anything about it. His mouth was sweet and I actually found myself enjoying this so much more than I thought I would.

What the fuck was I even doing? I asked myself, falling deeper and deeper into this moment, enjoying it a lot more than I should, and making myself look like a fool, too.

After all, I could already see it. I could already see Yanric rubbing it in my face how much he had always been right.

We continued to make out for what felt like an eternity and Yanric didn't even slide his tongue between my lips – at least, not yet.

He was enjoying this, dragging this moment out for as long as he could.

I was breathless. For a moment, I thought that we were going to keep making out until I was suffocating.

But that wasn't what happened. After a moment, he broke the kiss by pulling his head back, his eyes holding me and studying my facial expression.

I hated myself. I hated that I fell so easily into his trap without being able to do anything about it. Now, it was too late and he had all the reasons to think that all my repulsion of him was nothing more than bullshit.

"You kiss well for an amateur," he said, joking.

"Shut up," I said, folding my arms over my chest.

"Are you going to tell me that you didn't like it?" He asked, still smirking. And I could feel the difference in his scent. He enjoyed it, too, and probably a lot more than he should.

What was I going to say? I felt that whatever I said, I would still find myself in the same corner, trapped.

"I'm not going to answer that."

"Yes, you're going to answer my question," he insisted.

Blushing, I said, "do you think we could do it again just so that I can tell that for sure?" I asked, wondering if I should do it or not.

But I'd already said it, so there was nothing I could do to change my words.

He chuckled, silence around us. Nothing more than that. It was so quiet that I could even hear his breathing.

"Oh boy, I already knew you were going to say that," he joked, connecting his lips with mine, and this time we started to make out more slowly and sensually. It wasn't as passionate as the first kiss, probably because the novelty had already worn off.

Just like last time, I was breathless, and I could only kick myself for brushing off this kind of experience. I didn't kiss anyone this whole time since my teenage years because I was a mental wreck and shy as fuck.

It was something I couldn't do anything about.

Growing bolder, Yanric slid his tongue between my lips, and just like last time, I was unable to do anything about it. Actually,

I wanted his tongue sliding there and battling with mine for domination. It wasn't much of a fight, though. In no time at all, he had full control of the smooch and could do anything he wanted.

Still, Yanric was responsible and the moment he noticed I was breathless again, he pulled back, holding me with his gaze just like the first time.

"So, what do you say?" He asked, his voice sexier than normal. "Did you like it?"

I blushed. After all, what other reaction could I be having right now after he kissed me so tenderly?

There was something else crossing my mind. I imagined myself not only losing the virginity of my mouth, but also something else.

"I just want to say that it doesn't mean anything. I was just curious."

"You didn't answer my question," he persisted, annoying me slightly about it.

"I really don't know-" I was saying but he cut me off again, holding up his hand. Every time that I was going to say I didn't know what he was talking about, he did that now.

"Oh, come on. I've already told you that you are only lying to yourself by saying something like that. It really is pathetic."

"I don't know what else to say..." I eventually let out, feeling shame.

I mean, what else was I going to say? I asked myself, feeling stupid as much as I hated myself.

"I think you know exactly what to say," Yanric said, his hand going under the blanket. That was what I wanted, but I didn't know if I was ready for it.

At least, not yet.

I took a deep breath in. Perhaps it was something I needed to admit, even though I didn't know if I was ready for it.

"I liked it. I liked the kiss, the way that you did that with your lips," I said, smiling softly.

I didn't even know how to admit that without hurting myself in the process. Every time I thought I was making progress in coming to terms with this, I felt I was only lying to myself.

"Good. That's exactly what I thought, too," he murmured, leaning down and nibbling on my earlobe, though only gently and momentarily. As soon as he got what he wanted, he pulled back.

In the meantime, his hand was still going under my blanket, and I felt my heart rate speeding up. I could do everything to stop him from continuing, but I didn't do it, considering that so many things could go wrong… and right at the same time.

This was weird.

"What are you going to do, Yanric?" I asked, holding his gaze even though it was difficult to continue doing so. After all, I could already feel his hand on my thigh.

He was looking for my cock. This was making me wet, and I couldn't do anything about it without ruining it, which sucked.

Okay, so say I wanted this to continue. What would happen later was someone stepping inside the hut and finding him doing this. Then, we would both be kicked out of here, something I couldn't even think about without it hurting me.

"I've been thinking about doing this with you for such a long time," he admitted, sliding his hand under my pants. I now wished he was taking off my pants instead of looking for my prick.

I couldn't do anything about this because I was consenting to it, the heat emanating from my body telling him everything he wanted to know about this.

"Gosh, you are so fucking hard right now," he murmured, sliding his fingers around my hardness, and I couldn't hold the moan that escaped my lips.

Was this really going to continue? I asked myself, my entire body trembling. I knew that touching my dick could shower me with pleasure, but I didn't think it was so strong.

I felt as though it was dominating my entire body.

"Fuck," I muttered when he gave my cock a pump, his eyes still only looking at me. Yanric was still smirking, and I doubted that anyone could erase it from his face.

"This feels so good," he said before starting to pump my dick over and over, sliding his hand up and down on it for what felt like an eternity, and I could already feel it happening.

I could already feel my orgasm coming up. When it finally washed over me, I would have no option but to let him undress me and change my pants with his. After all, when this was over, my cum would add to the stench coming from the lower part of my body and I didn't want to reek even more.

And Yanric only continued to pump my dick, increasing his pace when he grew more certain about what he was doing and how to proceed.

I closed my eyes when I felt it happening. My climax was strong and jaw-dropping, making my entire body shake with pleasure. What's more, my cum shot out of my dick in thick, long ropes which smeared the blanket and my pants.

I didn't even have time to take it off until it was too late.

CHAPTER 8

Yanric

I did imagine that this was going to happen, but I was still surprised by the speed it was all unraveling. My hand was still around his prick, enjoying the cum on it. I didn't want to move it anywhere, just taking in this moment.

"Seeing you now tells me that you are enjoying this a lot more than you thought you were going to," I said, making that obvious.

I mean, what else was I going to say? It was everything I thought it was going to be and a lot more than that, too.

"I shouldn't be saying this, but you hit the nail on the head. That is exactly what I'm thinking," he said, smiling. I didn't know this for sure, but it felt like it was the first time he was smiling with me.

"See? I told you it wasn't going to be so bad," I joked, brushing my hand over his gland. He was still hard and I had to do something about that, though maybe not here. We needed our own place where we could have privacy after he was feeling better. After all, I didn't want to hurt him.

I didn't hurt him when he fell into that ravine, but sometimes that thought crossed my mind. Blaming myself was a hobby, I thought while holding a chuckle.

"It was really so good," he said, still basking in the pleasure that I showered his body with.

"I'm glad you think that way about it."

He took a deep breath, biting his bottom lip. Now was my time to ask the most important question floating in my mind.

"Do you want to stay with me forever?"

He turned his head to me slowly, for now not saying anything. I knew it was a pretty difficult question for him to answer, but I felt that he still needed to give me his thoughts about it.

"I don't know. I just don't really see myself living in this place."

"What's so wrong about this island that you hate so much?" I insisted.

He shrugged. "I don't know. Every time I think about this, I imagine myself living on the continent, learning how to drive, living in a cozy and simple apartment, and meeting new people. That's the kind of life I want."

I sighed, wishing he hadn't said that. I did think he was going to say those words, but I had still grown hopeful his mind was going to be more malleable.

"I see," I said, moving my hand from under the blanket. There was no point in continuing this anymore, unless I changed my mind about it, deciding to go to the continent with him.

We could do that...

I only had to change my mind about it and we would do it, but... I still didn't want to leave the island. When I thought about my future, I imagined it materializing right here and not in another place.

It sucked so much that I couldn't do anything about that.

"Wait, what are you doing?" Wadyn asked, sounding surprised by this. I mean, what did he think was going to happen now? Did he think that I was going to continue this knowing that we couldn't be husband and husband?

"Nothing. Nothing is exactly what I should have started to do from the beginning," I grumbled, standing up. "And I have to wipe off your cum now."

I padded over to the bucket with water, grabbed a washcloth, soaked it in the water, and then I wiped my hand clean. No more of his cum on my hand, which should be making me feel something, but it didn't.

"Just like that?" He asked, still sounding surprised. I was so disappointed that I didn't even know what I thought was going to happen. Maybe I had really thought he was going to change his mind and would choose to continue living here on the island, but… I was only fooling myself.

"Just like that…" I said, coming back to him, but without looking into his eyes. I knew that if I looked into his eyes, I would see how disappointed he was in me. He was in the right, of course. I also felt disappointed in myself, and there was nothing I could do about it.

I lifted the blanket and then the upper part of his pants, removing as much of his cum as I could. Some had fallen on his pants and mixed with the material, so there wasn't much I could do about it.

Again, I remembered that now Wadyn was probably going to need a change of pants - much more so than before.

When I was done, I tossed the washcloth into a bin, going over to the entrance of the hut.

"Wait, don't go," he pleaded, making me stop. Even though I felt the loss of momentum I thought I was having, I wasn't going to be an ass.

I still thought he was my fated mate, but if there wasn't much I could do to change his mind, what was the point?

"What is it?" I asked, hoping that he was going to go straight to the point and not waste my time. I was done wasting my time with anyone.

Even though I never thought I would say this, maybe… I should look for someone else.

"I just want to say that I really enjoyed it."

That was it? That was everything he wanted to say? After all the trouble I went through, all the sacrifice, and pretty much everything else that came with looking after him, he only had that to tell me?

I felt like he only used me for his own benefit and now he discarded me, which was… Silly.

"Seriously?" I said, raising my hands and pointing them to my chest, trying to show how disappointed I was at his words. "That's everything you have to say?"

He widened his eyes. "Why are you being so mean all of a sudden?"

I put my hand on my forehead. "You know, if there is something I never thought you were, it was how dense you can be sometimes."

"Me being dense? You don't know what you're talking about. I'm not being dense. I said that I really enjoyed you giving me a handjob and kissing me. Maybe we could do those things again some more times in the future."

I waved my hand. "Sorry, Wadyn, but I don't think we'll be able to."

"Why not?" He asked, glancing down. "No matter how much I try to think things might be different, I don't think they will ever be, so I'll most likely stay stuck here on this goddamn island."

I took a deep breath in, finding his words so infuriating. "You know, I don't know what you think you're doing, but I still have no idea why you hate our island so much."

"I just imagine myself living a life bigger than this. Maybe with a partner, but no more than that."

"You might as well go and try your best to make that happen, then," I said, strutting out of the hut. I was done with that. I was done with Wadyn and even if he came back telling me he was sorry about it, it wouldn't change anything.

I was now outside of the hut, closing my eyes and basking in the familiar territory that was here. The trees, the residents of the village mingling, laughs, chatters, and that sort of thing. It was relaxing, to say the least.

Looking over my shoulder, I didn't imagine myself going back to the hut. To be honest, I wouldn't have to, considering that my father was around and he was the healer, so he could look after Wadyn until he didn't need our help anymore.

After that, I would tell him the truth, confirming that the marriage wasn't going to happen anymore.

But hey… what the hell was I thinking, considering that I was never one to give up? I asked myself, still stepping away from the hut. No matter how much Wadyn hated me, it wasn't going to change who I was.

Maybe we could strike a deal so that we could do both things. Maybe I could do that so that we could be together.

It was a possibility, one that renewed my hopes, or at least that was what I thought. Still walking away from the hut, I found myself now in the middle of the forest, going back to the place where he fell into the ravine. When he had fallen there, I thought that I had lost him, but thankfully he had only hurt himself.

He'd gotten lucky, to say the least.

"Wadyn, what the hell do you think you're doing with your life?" I asked myself, murmuring. I was only talking to myself, but it felt like I was talking to him.

Anyway, he was still my fated mate, even if I had thought we would never end up together, considering how much he wanted to move to the continent.

Going around the ravine, I stepped out of the forest and found myself on the beach, where I could see the lights and the buildings in the distance. That was where the continent was and where Wadyn wanted to go so much, to the point that he couldn't even see I was his fated mate.

CHAPTER 9

Wadyn

I was back home. I thought that Yanric was going to come back and say he was sorry for the way he treated me, but that had been nothing more than an illusion. He didn't come back and I had to see his father every time, something that hurt my heart a lot more than I thought it ever would.

We were doing something that shattered all my expectations, and I thought it meant so much to him that he would see beyond his 'marrying his fated mate' thing.

At least, that was what I hoped, but now I realized I was only being a fool. From this moment onward, it was obvious that Yanric didn't like me that much. He certainly had never been in love with me.

He only thought that I was his fated mate, and I couldn't believe that my father had gone along with it. It was such a crazy thing, now that I was thinking about it.

I took a deep breath in, remembering the kiss and his handjob. They composed an experience I would never forget, and that was putting it mildly.

It would never happen again, though.

I didn't think I would ever even see him again.

Turning around, I could see the disappointment on my father's face. He was sitting at the table, knitting. He was making a shirt for me. He said that I needed new shirts, considering that most of the other shirts I had were dirty and worn.

His eyes held me where I was, and I could tell he knew what I was thinking about.

"You're still thinking about him, aren't you?" He asked. "When I found my fated Alpha, I didn't think it was going to happen. I thought it was silly, too, but then I realized it was everything I wanted. He showed me how wrong I was about my wishes and dreams."

"How can you say something like that? How can you say that you were wrong about your own dreams? It just doesn't make any sense," I argued. I did have my dream, and I wasn't going to give up on it.

Living on the continent was everything I wanted and I didn't think that would ever change.

"You know my history. You know what happened."

I knew everything that happened in my father's past, but I still didn't want to think it might happen to me as well.

"Things were different back then. You didn't realize that the continent was such a good place to live in."

"I would argue that it's still not a good place for us, no matter how much you think otherwise."

"Do you really think that there is so much xenophobia over there?" I asked, seeing the continent even from here. The lights, the high-rises, and the other tall buildings… It was all alluring, to say the least.

"Not only do I know that, I know that it's much worse. When you get there – if you go there – people won't accept you initially. Not to mention that we all know that Yanric is your fated mate. Without him, you will always feel that something's missing."

"And then he would die just like my other father…" I murmured, not wishing to dive into that issue right now, but still finding it difficult, considering that my father just didn't want to let go.

There was this… thing that Alphas needed to do. Most people around here thought that it was just part of the culture, but for me, it was something else.

It was a reason for me to come to the conclusion that I couldn't marry and build my life here. Not ever.

He shot up from the chair he was sitting on, his eyes growing fierce. "Wadyn, don't ever say something like that to me."

"Why? Just because I was telling the truth?" I shouted, jumping out of our hut. I wasn't going to argue with my father, no matter how much part of me wanted to do that.

I couldn't stop them from coming out. The tears. They were coming out and rolling down my cheeks. My father couldn't see me like this, or else he would only insist that he was right.

He would tell me that I was crying because I was going against my own nature, which was silly.

Anyway, I decided to bolt into the forest again, but this time I wasn't running away from anyone. I jumped over a log and continued to run as far away from my village as possible, all the while looking for one thing – getting as close to the continent as possible.

It was almost there.

Seconds later, my feet came to a halt. Here I was. The beach. As close to the continent as I could get without going into the water. I didn't like it, just like most people here on this island didn't.

In fact, it was much more than that, too. I feared the water, the liquid moving lazily, sloshing on the shore, creating little waves. The more I thought about it, the more I wished I lived all the way in the middle of the continent, where there wasn't as much water as there was here.

"I didn't think I was going to find you here," his voice echoed from behind me, catching me off guard. I didn't think he was going to show up, much less tonight. I turned around in an instant, finding him with his hands in his pockets and looking at me with concerned eyes.

"What are you doing here around my village?" I asked, barking. Whatever he thought he was doing, I didn't like it. Maybe he was stalking me, something that I wouldn't put past him.

"I came here to say something I usually don't."

"And what thing is that?" I asked, feeling curious about this. Whatever he had to say to me, it was worth hearing him out.

CHAPTER 10

Yanric

I never thought it was going to happen, but here I stood, on the beach, seeing the continent in the distance. I looked over my shoulder and saw his village, the trees, and the animals that lived in the forest. I had really thought that living here was the right thing for me, but without my fated mate, who also rejected me, there was only one thing I could do.

Only one thing that completed me.

"I'm going to go with you to the continent. It's already been decided."

Wadyn widened his eyes. After all, he never thought I would say something like that, much less while showing so much certainty with my eyes.

"What?" He asked, sounding surprised. "After everything you've told me, now you want to go to the continent with me? What's going on with you?"

He took a couple of steps in my direction, approaching me.

"I've made up my mind about it. That's what's happening," I replied, the tone of my voice echoing how casual I was being about this.

He curled up the corner of his lips, still looking baffled by this. "I don't understand."

I approached him, putting my hand on his waist. His skin was so soft. I could feel it even through his shirt.

"The only thing you need to understand is that I'm willing to do everything just so that we are together. We don't have to marry. We don't have to follow the traditions of this island and we don't have to do anything else that doesn't mean us living together. Right now, it's the only thing I want," I insisted, this moment dragging out a little too long.

It was painful as much as it was revealing.

"Yanric, I don't even know what to say," he admitted and I put my finger on his lips, stopping him from saying anything else.

"You don't need to say anything. Do you want to do it? Do you want to go with me to the continent? Then, when we get there, you can finally show me how cars work and what it's like to fly in a plane."

His eyes shone with wonder and happiness, and he couldn't help but hug me, burying his head in my chest. This was everything I wanted. I put my hands on his head, and then I moved them around it, cupping his chin. Lifting his head up, I held him with my gaze while I locked my eyes with his.

A moment of nothingness and then... we kissed. We started to make out where everybody could see us, and I couldn't care less about that.

Most people would think it meant that Wadyn had let go of his dreams. That was okay. It meant the opposite of that.

His lips were as sweet and tender as the last time I kissed them, and it couldn't be any different. I didn't tell Wadyn this, but I missed this so much.

We continued to kiss for what felt like an eternity, and then he pulled his head back, just looking at me. He told me a lot through his stare, and I could tell that he wished we could do so much more right now.

But there was the thing about privacy and that we shouldn't do this on the beach, out in the open.

"But how are we going to do it?" He asked, his reasons for being puzzled by this all too understandable. "I mean, we don't even have a boat, and I'm pretty sure that the only few the island have are under your father's control."

"We'll just steal one," I replied, noticing the change in his scent. He never thought that I would suggest stealing a boat.

He cocked his eyebrow, saying, "you are kidding, right? You're not going to steal a boat. I know how much you are faithful to this island and the people that live here. You would never forgive yourself if you did that."

"You actually don't know much about me," I said, kissing him one more time. This time, I didn't stop myself before sliding my tongue between his lips, just basking at this moment as much as I could.

By the time we were done kissing, Wadyn was breathless. I took all the air that was in his lungs, and that was putting it mildly.

"I missed this so much," he said, grabbing my hand. After that, we began to walk to the other side of the island, where all the boats were. It was going to take some time to get there, but we knew that we could make it, and then we would steal one of them.

Easy peasy, at least for me. I was one of the few who guarded the place where the boats were, so I knew how to open it. Plus, I had the key and everything.

It wouldn't be so difficult. It wouldn't even be the most difficult thing I did in my life. I'd done much worse and things much riskier, to say the least.

Wadyn flicked his eyes up, finding me. "But after we get there, what do you think will happen? We don't have anywhere to stay, and we don't have money. We don't even have anyone that could help us get through the most difficult things."

He was right about that. We didn't have that at all, and that was putting it mildly. I didn't know how it would happen, and I was certain that we would face some hardships, but it was still better than not being with my fated mate.

Stroking his cheek, I said, "don't worry about it. We'll figure something out when we get there."

He didn't say anything and, for the time being, he didn't even know what else to say. I could just imagine what he was thinking and feeling right now. It was like he wasn't himself anymore, walking like a ghost.

He didn't need to worry, though. Everything was going to go well for us.

WADYN'S EPILOGUE

Here I was, on the continent and on the balcony of my apartment overlooking the city and what was beyond it. I had seen this place so many times when I was on the island, never imagining that one day I would find myself here.

My partner was behind me. He was still mounting the wardrobe we bought. A wardrobe. We didn't have to pile up our clothes in a corner anymore, I thought with happiness filling me.

So many things from the island we didn't have to do anymore. The quality of life on the continent was miles better.

I could hear Yanric hammering the nails on the wood boards that composed the wardrobe, most likely making much more noise than the neighbors were used to. Chances were that, tomorrow, we would get some mean letters about it.

Brushing that aside, I couldn't care less about it.

I closed my eyes and basked at this moment, enjoying it so much more than anything that ever happened before in my life. We hadn't been here long yet and we were still building our life here, but I had already begun to wonder if we couldn't... Marry. I mean, there were some things to fix and resolve before that, but for the time being, I could just imagine it happening.

He would put the ring on my finger and would call me his husband. I could even imagine a life with kids and a couple of other things, if only we could also have enough money and more space for them.

At least, that was how I looked at it. I didn't want to make the same mistake that my parents did, putting me into this life without imagining how I would live in it. They never once wondered what I would want for my life when I was an adult.

Opening my eyes, I remembered that it was all in the past, and all I could focus on was what was going to happen in the future.

Was I imagining things or did Yanric just stop hammering the wardrobe? I asked myself the moment I felt his arms going around my torso, cupping my belly. A moment following that, he landed his lips on my neck, giving it a long and profound kiss. Squirming, I turned my head up, finding his eyes and saying, "I love you so much. I never thought I would say this when we were still on the island, but now that I think about it, I just love you so much that I can't imagine spending a minute of my life without you."

"I also never thought you would say something like that," he confessed, kissing me one more time, and this time it was on my lips, making me arch my back. I turned around in his arms, and then I put my arms around him, kissing him one more time. This time, our kiss was much more tender and stronger than the last one, and I made some promises I didn't even know I would ever be able to keep.

YANRIC'S EPILOGUE

I found myself sitting on the couch, holding a piece of paper in my hand. I had it because I was thinking about what I was going to write to my father. After all, I stole that boat and didn't even yet say that I was sorry about it. I knew he hated me. He always thought that I was going to follow tradition and continue it, but I decided to do this crazy thing, living with an Omega that didn't want to be on the island anymore.

Anyway, I had to write something.

Just when I put the tip of the pen on the paper, a pair of hands settled on my shoulders, making me snap my head up. It was Wadyn, his smile widening.

"What are you doing, my love?" He asked, his hands now cupping my neck. His skin was soft as ever, and I could feel the warmth coming from his body and even the change in his scent.

The interesting thing was that I was so immersed in what I was doing I didn't even notice his scent when he was coming. Not to mention that, here on the continent, there were so many people and so many scents that it was difficult to single his out.

"I need to write a letter to my father. I need to tell him what happened. I know he already knows, but he still needs to hear it from me."

He took a deep breath. Wadyn never liked my dad, but there was nothing he could do about this. This was personal.

"Do you really have to write him anything?" He asked, kissing my right cheek. "He never liked you enough to understand what you wanted."

I kissed him on the lips, saying, "he liked me a lot, much more so than you think. I'm not doing this just for him, though. I'm doing this for myself as well."

A moment of silence hung in the air, and I couldn't help but wonder what else he was going to say.

He waved his hand. "Fine. Write to him that you are happy with me and that there is nothing he can do to change that. Not to mention that he has another son, so if he wants to continue the tradition, he can have it through him."

He was right about that. There was still my brother and he was even more adamant about following the tradition, which would eventually lead him to his death. I had once thought that I would die in the glorious battle that came with all of that, but now I realized it was kind of stupid.

"I'm certainly going to write to him that we are happy together," I confirmed and then I added, "I love you so much."

"And I love you too, my promised Alpha."

The End

Looking for more books like this one? Check these out:

1. Omega's Possessive Alpha
2. Alpha's Surrogate Omega
3. Alpha's Shy Omega

Don't forget to leave your review. It really helps me!

TEASER: OMEGA'S POSSESSIVE ALPHA

MPREG Wolf Shifter Romance (Alpha MC - 1)

Look, it didn't really matter how much my father wanted to make this happen, it wasn't going to. Even though the party was energetic, it wasn't going to make me fall for the cocky guy standing across from me all the way on the other side of the main hall.

"He's just so much older than me. There is no way that there can ever be a relationship between us," I said to my best friend. Draco was standing here with me and he was a member of the pack.

Even though I would never say this, the truth was that I would rather be in a romantic relationship with him than with Lux. I mean, it just wouldn't really work.

Although, I couldn't help but admit that he was quite the eye candy. He was fit. His body was sculpted, his muscles showing even though he was wearing a dark suit. It didn't really fit him, though. I just had no idea what he even thought he was doing here at this party.

"Does age really matter that much? I mean, he is only 30 years old and you are 21. It's about time you started to go to college or just do something with your life. I'm in college, and I really enjoy it."

Draco tried to smile, but he wasn't really fooling anyone here. He didn't actually enjoy attending classes and whatever else he thought he was doing in college. As for me, my career was focused on something else. I was focused on becoming a developer. A programmer. That was what I was focused on and nothing would change that.

I took a sip from the wineglass I was holding. Grimacing, I just really couldn't understand why people thought that wine tasted good. It just didn't.

"It matters to me. I'm not going to begin a relationship with anyone just because my father wants it. Not to mention that he still thinks there is something as ridiculous as 'fated mates.' Just thinking about it, I feel like I'm going to puke."

And yet, my eyes couldn't stop glancing to the left and stealing glances at him. I had no idea what I was even doing. If Lux noticed that I was stealing glances at him, he would certainly take the next step and come to me.

"I just think that you are wrong about this. You should go and talk to him at least. It can't really hurt," he said as he winked. I rolled my eyes and then began to walk away. Where to? I didn't know. Anywhere that wasn't the main hall was good enough for me.

In a moment, I found myself outside, and here I could breathe and think about everything going on in my life. There was this pressure on me to marry and find my partner, even though it was ridiculous.

I sat down on a chair by the swimming pool. I couldn't deny that I was spoiled. My house was more like a mansion. It was big and fancy, and I knew a lot of people would give almost everything they had to live the rest of their lives here.

At least, that was what I was telling myself anyway. I was just trying to make myself feel better about my current, shitty situation.

The air around me was fresh and calming. I inhaled it slowly while still thinking about Lux. What was about him that kept on making my mind go back to him all the time?

Maybe it was his impossibly blue eyes and his manly scent. I was an Omega, so I could smell him without difficulty even from a distance, just like now. Even though he was still in the main hall, I could smell him. And it was really like he was right behind me.

"I saw you coming here," his voice echoed behind me. I shot up from where I was sitting while whirling around and meeting his eyes as they continued to stare at me. I never thought that he would show up all of a sudden when I was trying to think about anything that didn't involve him.

"What are you doing here?" I asked as I raised my voice. It was like I was begging for someone to help me. Maybe Draco would come, but I didn't think so. He was probably mingling with the other partygoers right now.

"I needed some fresh air, so I came outside. Nothing more than that, really. It certainly doesn't mean that I wanted to talk to you in person." He smirked after saying that. Of course he was going to do that. Lux was so convinced about the effect he was having on me.

I took a few steps away from him. He wasn't going to fool me now no matter what happened.

"Stay away from me!" I shouted. This time, I did that while hoping that at least one of the partygoers would hear it. Whether that would happen or not, we were going to find out in the next couple of seconds.

But… There was only gentle music coming from the main hall. Nobody heard anything, which made me feel even more paralyzed than I was right now.

My cock was hard. There was no denying it. If there was something I wanted to make happen right now, it was this Alpha manhandling me the way that I knew he could. He would put me right back in my place and then he would kiss me. I could just imagine how soft his lips were.

But I shouldn't even be thinking that. He could read my mind. I was certain he could do that.

He lifted his hands and put them in front of him as though he was making a stop sign. "All right, all right. You don't need to worry about that. I'm not going to do anything to you that you don't want."

After a moment of silence, I realized that he wasn't going to harm me or try to touch me without my consent. Where was everybody? I asked myself, realizing how stupid I was being about this. The truth was that I was still in my house and, given that, Lux had to get out of here if I said so to the guards.

MPREG SERIES AND MORE

SERIES - OMEGAVERSE MC

1. Omega for Obsessive Alpha
2. Omega for Protective Alpha
3. Omega for Jealous Alpha

SERIES - PREGNANT FOR HIM

1. Controlled by the Alpha 1: An MPREG Omegaverse Story
2. Controlled by the Alpha 2: An MPREG Omegaverse Story
3. Controlled by the Alpha 3: Dominating the Fertile Omega
4. Controlled by the Alpha 4: An Omega's Tale of Obedience
5. Controlled by the Alpha 5: A Tale of Obedient Submission
6. Controlled by the Alpha 6: Monopolized in Outer Space

SERIES - LOST INNOCENCE

1. Overwhelming the Omega 1: His Little Doll
2. Overwhelming the Omega 2: Brute Entry and Double Teamed
3. Overwhelming the Omega 3: His Tight Backdoor
4. Overwhelming the Omega 4: Stretching his Front Door
5. Overwhelming the Omega 5: Until he Spasms
6. Overwhelming the Omega 6: Naïve and Untouched

ABOUT THE AUTHOR

Steamy MM stories, baby! Michael Levi can't go a day without sitting down and putting into words all the dirty scenes that sprout in his mind. His collection is diverse, but it's gay love only. And if you are looking for something free, check his mailing list. Warning: it can be extra spicy.

When Michael Levi isn't writing, he's chilling out by the lake close to his house. Nothing better than kicking back with a martini in his hand as he daydreams his next explicit scenes.

9 798359 610377